Bubble Trouble

For Katie and Euan

Find out more about **Ricky Rocket** at
www.shoo-rayner.co.uk

First published in 2006 by Orchard Books
First paperback publication in 2007

ORCHARD BOOKS
338 Euston Road, London NW1 3BH
Orchard Books Australia
Hachette Children's Books
Level 17/207 Kent St, Sydney, NSW 2000

ISBN-10: 1 84616 039 1 (hardback)
ISBN-13: 978 1 84616 039 4 (hardback)

ISBN-10: 1 84616 394 3 (paperback)
ISBN-13: 978 1 84616 394 4 (paperback)

Text and illustrations © Shoo Rayner 2006

A CIP catalogue record for this book is available from the British Library.

1 3 5 7 9 10 8 6 4 2 (hardback)
1 3 5 7 9 10 8 6 4 2 (paperback)

Printed in Great Britain

Orchard Books is a division of Hachette Children's Books.

Bubble Trouble

Shoo Rayner

ORCHARD BOOKS

Ricky Rocket, the only Earth boy on the planet of Hammerhead, was fed up. "It's so unfair," he growled. "Why does Granny Earth have to stay in my room on Candlenight?"

Ricky's little sister, Sue, pointed at
him. "You're so selfish, Ricky!"

"Granny can sleep in your room, then!" Ricky snapped.

"My bed is far too small for Granny!" Sue said.

"Would you two stop it?" sighed Mum. "Candlenight is a celebration of peace with our friends and family."

"Huh!" Ricky grunted. "It'll be peaceful alright. Dad says we can't have fireworks."

"Fireworks would upset the neighbours," Dad explained patiently.

An idea wiggled its way into Ricky's brain.

"Mum?" he asked. "Can Bubbles join us for Candlenight?"

Mum eyed Ricky suspiciously.

"If Bubbles came," Ricky explained, "we could sleep out in the tent and Granny Earth could have my room to herself."

8

Mum couldn't think of any
reason to say no, so she got on
the communicator to arrange
things with Bubble's mum.

"Yippee!" Ricky cheered.

"Wow!" **Bubbles stood** wide-eyed
in the middle of the living room.
"It's amazing!"

The house was full of candles and decorations. Tiny lights twinkled on a tinsel tree that was hung with gold and silver balls.

"Back on Earth," Ricky's gran explained, "there's a time called Winterval, when the nights are long and dark. The longest night is Candlenight. That's when we have a party."

"A proper Candlenight party ends
with fireworks," Ricky grumbled.
"But Dad won't let us have any."

"Your father is right to think
of the neighbours," said Granny.
"This is a time to think of others."

13

"Sometimes, people give presents on Candlenight!" Ricky hinted.

"Oh yes!" Gran laughed. "Here you are, Ricky – Happy Candlenight!"

Ricky tore the shiny paper
off a huge parcel.

"Woo-ee!" he shrieked. "The
Lord Vorg Laser Blazer 3000^{SR}!
Thanks, Gran!"

Ricky set the Laser Blazer up and pressed the trigger. A glowing bolt of light shot across the room. The Laser Blazer screen exploded in colour.

"Almost as good as fireworks!" Ricky whooped.

"Urgh! Sprouts!" Ricky and Sue groaned.

"Mmmm!" Bubbles enthused. "They look delicious!"

"Good for you, Bubbles." Dad said. "Eat as much as you like!"

Bubbles piled his plate high with sprouts and chestnuts and cabbage and bean stew and fried artichokes. He had three helpings, and drank four cans of Fizzywizzy^{SR}.

After two helpings of Candle
Pudding, a handful of brandy snaps,
extra whipped cream, custard, fruit,
nuts and cheese and biscuits, he
had just enough room left for the
minty chocolates.

Bubbles burped. "That was fantastic,
Mrs Rocket!"

Then the trouble began.

CANDLENIGHT SUPPER

The centrepiece of a
Candlenight Supper
is the **Lurkey**.

Lurkey is made from
vegetable protein that
has been **woven** and **knitted** into
the shape of a large, cooked bird.

Fried artichokes (fartichokes)
are a **Candlenight*** favourite.

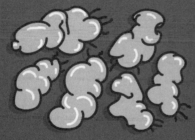

These unusually
shaped vegetables
can have an **instant
effect** on some
digestive systems.

Party hats are **essential.**
They come in **crackers.** No one can
remember where this tradition comes from.

*****Read
A Present from Earth
for more about Candlenight.

An orange bubble slipped out of one
of Bubble's trumpets. Bubbles blushed.
Everyone pretended that they hadn't
seen it.

More bubbles escaped, and drifted
towards the candles on the table.
When they hit the flames, they burst
with a loud POP!

23

Ricky clapped his hands.
"Indoor fireworks!" he laughed.
"Do it again, Bubbles!"

"Ricky!" Mum hissed. "Behave!"
Ricky couldn't help himself.
He kept giggling.

Sue started giggling too. The air filled with the kind of ear-splitting, blood-curdling, brain-jamming shrieks that little Earth girls are famous for all over the universe.

A stream of orange bubbles shot out of Bubbles. They floated round the house, popping at every candle.

"This is the best Candlenight ever!"
Ricky screamed.

"Ricky! You're embarrassing your
friend," Mum said.

"Sorry, Mrs Rocket," Bubbles spluttered. "I can't help it. It must have been the sprouts – some things have a strange effect on Fuddle stomachs."

"You did eat a lot of them," Dad laughed. "But Candlenight is all about eating too much."

"And fireworks!" Ricky muttered darkly.

FUDDLES

Bubbles is a **Fuddle**. **They come** from the planet **Fuddleduddle.**

Fuddles are mostly gasbags, which is why they **float.** Excess gas is released from their trumpets as **bubbles.**

TRUMPET VALVE

STOMACH

GASBAG

Fuddle hands have **three sticky pads** to help them **hold on in a strong wind.**

Fuddles use their tentacules to move. It is still a mystery how this actually works!

Later, Ricky and Bubbles took turns to shoot down Lord Vorg's space fleet on the Laser Blazer screen.

A glowing orange bubble slowly drifted in front of the target. Ricky aimed at it and squeezed the trigger.

The bubble exploded
in a ball of blue flames.

Ricky whooped. "More!"

Bubbles squeezed out bubble after bubble, and Ricky shot them down in flames. They collapsed in a fit of giggles.

"That's enough!" Mum ordered.
"Go outside – get in that tent and
go to sleep! And you can leave that
toy in here!"

Ricky woke in a sweat. He'd dreamt he was in his rocket, being chased by the Evil Lord Vorg's battle cruiser.

Now that he was wide-awake, he still felt as if he was flying.

Bubbles snored and spluttered – bubbles still streamed out of his trumpets. "Phwoor! It stinks in here!" Ricky gasped.

He fought with the tent zip and forced his head outside. He gulped down a lungful of fresh air and took in the view.

"Quick, Bubbles!" he hissed. "Wake up! Abandon ship!"

The tent was floating three metres off the ground. The last tent peg strained to stop it flying away.

Ricky and Bubbles stared
at each other.

"Help!" they yelled.

EVIL LORD VORG'S
TOP THREE
LASER BLAZER GAMES

1. Target Practice (easy):
Shoot flying saucers before they take off.

2. Ambush in Sector 9 (hard):
Shoot your way through the robot army to escape and live another day.

3. Event Horizon (impossible):
The Evil Lord Vorg has a new and deadly weapon. Can you destroy it before he destroys you?

"OK, stay calm!" Dad ordered. "Jump, Bubbles. I'll catch you."

Dad was surprised at how light Bubbles was. "He must be full of wind!" he thought.

"Come on, Ricky. Quick!"

Ricky kicked around with his legs, waiting for Dad's hands to grab him.

"Jump, Ricky!" Dad shouted. "The rope's come free!"

Ricky closed his eyes and let go. Falling into Dad's arms, he saw the tent drift slowly upwards.

"How are we going to get the tent
down?" Bubbles gasped.

"Simple!" Ricky said.

He ran into the house and picked up the Laser Blazer 3000 [SR]. He lifted it up to his shoulder, shut one eye and zeroed in on the target.

LASER BLAZER 3000 TARGET-O-MATIC

"No-o-o-o-o!" Dad cried.

Too late. Ricky had pulled the trigger. A bolt of light hurtled towards the floating tent.

The tent exploded into a million pieces as an enormous bang knocked them off their feet. Tiny bits of burning cloth twinkled gold and silver as they fell through the night sky.

"Yippee!" Ricky cheered. "Now that's what I call a firework display! Happy Candlenight, everyone!"

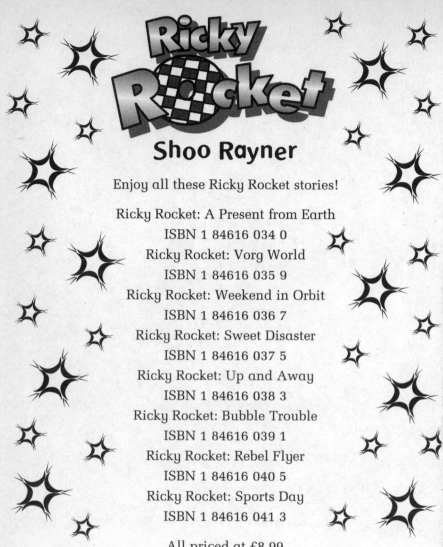

Ricky Rocket

Shoo Rayner

Enjoy all these Ricky Rocket stories!

All priced at £8.99

Orchard Crunchies are available from all good bookshops, or can be ordered
direct from the publisher: Orchard Books, PO BOX 29, Douglas IM99 1BQ
Credit card orders please telephone 01624 836000 or fax 01624 837033
or visit our internet site: www.wattspub.co.uk or e-mail: bookshop@enterprise.net for details.

To order please quote title, author and ISBN and your full name and address.
Cheques and postal orders should be made payable to 'Bookpost plc.'
Postage and packing is FREE within the UK
(overseas customers should add £1.00 per book).

Prices and availability are subject to change.